I Wish I'd Been Born a
Unicorn

by Rachel Lyon
Illustrated by Andrea Ringli

Mucky was a **playful** horse,
Who lived up to his name.
He didn't **bathe**, or brush his teeth,
And never **combed** his mane.

No other horse would share his field
Because he'd grown so **smelly**,
And **flies** and **fleas** would bite his knees
And picnic on his **belly**.

"I wish I had some friends," he sighed,
While chewing on some hay.
"But no one seems to like me much -
I'm never asked to play."

"If I'd been born a unicorn,
I bet they'd like me more.
But I'm just silly Mucky,
Who likes rolling on the floor."

"Your true friends," said a clever owl
As Mucky ate his meal,
"Aren't bothered how you look or smell,
But only how you feel."

"However, if it's really what you want,
I'll make your wish come true.
I'll help you be a unicorn."
And up and off he flew.

Now, unicorns are white, of course,
And Mucky's brown and plain.
So first, Owl asked the cows for milk
To paint his coat and mane.

"But milk is runny," mooed the cows.
"It simply will not stick!
Perhaps if Frog will swim around,
He'll churn it nice and thick."

Owl headed next towards the beach,
To find a **pointy** shell,
Which once tied tight on Mucky's head
Would work so very well.

Owl took the **cream** to Mucky's field
And worked the whole night through.
He turned him white from head to hoof,
To make his **dream** come true.

One final touch, between his ears,
He tied the **seashell horn**.
"Come look," Owl cried to all around.
"And see the **unicorn!**"

Up hurried frog, the cows came too,
They waited in the field.
The sun came up and in its light,
New Mucky was revealed.

"A unicorn? Where?" Mucky asked.
"You surely don't mean me?"
"Oh yes," Frog and the cows replied.
"Look in the pond, you'll see."

"I am! I am a **unicorn**!"
He sang and skipped with glee.
"I'll soon have friends, and best of all,
They'll want to play with me."

But **suddenly** a cloud appeared.
It slid across the **sun**.
"It mustn't rain!" thought Little Owl.
"Poor Mucky's coat will run."

The sky grew **dark**, the wind blew **wild**,
The raindrops tumbled down.
And right before their very eyes
The unicorn turned brown.

"Oh deary me," the milk cows cried.
"Poor Mucky seemed so glad,
But now the milk's been washed away,
He looks so very sad."

"Dear Mucky, please don't cry", they begged.
"We'll make more **cream** today,
And once you're painted white again,
We're sure you'll get to **play**."

But as they looked on, feeling sad,
They saw a smile appear.
It grew on Mucky's dirty face
From filthy ear to ear.

"Who needs to be a unicorn?
Who needs a wish come true?
I'll never feel alone again
With friends as good as you!"

"It's like Owl promised yesterday -
You know your friends are **real**
When all they truly care about
Is how you really feel."

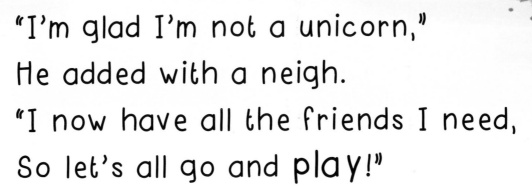

"I'm glad I'm not a unicorn,"
He added with a neigh.
"I now have all the friends I need,
So let's all go and play!"

The End

I Wish I'd Been Born a Unicorn
is an original concept by © Rachel Lyon

Author: Rachel Lyon

Illustrator: Andrea Ringli

Published by MAVERICK ARTS PUBLISHING LTD
Studio 3A, City Business Centre, 6 Brighton Road,
Horsham, West Sussex, RH13 5BB
© Maverick Arts Publishing Limited May 2018 [Second Edition] +44 (0)1403 256941

A CIP catalogue record for this book is available at the British Library.

ISBN 978-1-84886-329-3

Maverick
arts publishing
www.maverickbooks.co.uk